Written by **Taye Diggs**   Illustrated by **Shane W. Evans**

A Conversation about Race

WHY...

are those buildings burning?

Feiwel & Friends
New York

"Yes, my sweet boy."

"Why are those people shouting?"

"Our people are shouting because we need to be heard. We need to be heard."

"OH."

"Our people are crying because we are in pain. We are in pain."

"OH."

"Nanna?"

"Yes, my grandson."

"Why are those people pointing?"

"Our people are pointing because we need help. We really need help."

"OH."

"**G**randad?"

"Yes, my lovely granddaughter."

"Why are those people marching?"

"Our people are marching because we have been stomped
on and stepped over for way too long. Way, way too long."

"OH."

The little children looked at
the brown skin staring back
in their reflections.

He saw the bright light
of fire through the window.

She could smell
the dark smoke.

"Why are those buildings burning?"

"Because, little one . . ."

"When we get tired of shouting
and not being heard,

when we have cried so many
tears from always getting hurt,

when we scream out for help
and continue to get ignored,

when we march and march and
march but are not really moving—

when all this happens . . ."

"Sometimes buildings must burn.

The buildings burn for us.

The anger burning those buildings is us."

The child then sat down
and crossed her legs.
He closed his eyes.

"Why are you
praying, little one?"
they all asked.

"I'm praying for faith and love.

If we have that, then maybe we can figure this all out—maybe then we will have peace.

Yes. I believe we will figure this out."

So they all sat down and closed their eyes.
And prayed.

They all prayed for peace.

To Walker and all the young ones. —T.D.

Thanks to the Most High Love!
Thank God for the gift. Dedicated to my loving
family. To the Little Ones: Be in Joy. —S.W.E.

A FEIWEL AND FRIENDS BOOK
An imprint of Macmillan Publishing Group, LLC
120 Broadway, New York, NY 10271
mackids.com

Library of Congress Cataloging-in-Publication Data is available.

First edition, 2021
Book design by Mike Burroughs
The illustrations were created using digital collage, alkyd paint swatches, and a whole lot of love and patience.
Feiwel and Friends logo designed by Filomena Tuosto
Printed in China by RR Donnelley Asia Printing Solutions Ltd., Dongguan City, Guangdong Province.

ISBN 978-1-250-80609-3 (hardcover)
1 3 5 7 9 10 8 6 4 2